The Snowstorm

Written by Michèle Dufresne
Illustrated by Cula Carmen Elena

Contents

Pioneer Valley Educational Press, Inc.

The Snowstorm

"Look!" said Little Penguin.
"It's snowing!"

"I love snow,"
said Baby Seal.
"Let's go for a walk."

Little Penguin and Baby Seal
walked and walked
in the snow.

"Look! I can catch
a snowflake
with my tongue,"
said Baby Seal.

"I can, too,"
said Little Penguin.

4

"Look! I can make tracks
in the snow,"
said Baby Seal.

"I can, too,"
said Little Penguin.

"Oh, no! Where are we?
Are we lost?"
asked Baby Seal.

"Uh-oh,"
said Little Penguin.
"Where are we?"

Baby Seal began to cry.
"No one will find us,"
said Baby Seal.
"It's snowing. No one
can see us."

"No one can see us,
but they can hear us,"
Little Penguin told Baby Seal.
"We can call for help."

"Help!" called Baby Seal.

"Help! Help!"
called Little Penguin.

"I can hear Little Penguin
and Baby Seal
calling for help,"
said Mrs. Polar Bear.

"I can hear them, too,"
said Grandpa Walrus.
"They are in trouble again.
We must go
and find them."

Grandpa Walrus
and Mrs. Polar Bear
looked and looked for
Little Penguin and Baby Seal.

It was snowing harder
and harder.

"We must keep on calling,"
said Little Penguin.

"Help!" called Baby Seal.

"Help! Help!"
called Little Penguin.

"I can hear them!"
said Mrs. Polar Bear.
"Here they are!"

12

"You found us!"
said Baby Seal.

"Yes," said Mrs. Polar Bear.
"We could hear you
calling for help!"

The Snowstorm:
The Play

Look! It's snowing.

I love snow.
Let's go for a walk.

Little Penguin and
Baby Seal walked
and walked
in the snow.

 Look! I can catch a snowflake with my tongue.

 I can, too!

 Look! I can make tracks in the snow.

 I can, too!

Oh, no!
Where are we?
Are we lost?

Uh-oh!
Where are we?

No one will find us.
It's snowing. No one
can see us.

But they can
hear us.
Help!

 I can hear
Little Penguin
and Baby Seal
calling for help.

 Grandpa Walrus
and Mrs. Polar Bear
looked and looked
for Little Penguin
and Baby Seal.
It was snowing harder
and harder.

 Here they are!

 You found us!

Walruses

The walrus is a big animal that lives in cold places. The walrus and the seal belong to a group of animals called pinniped. Pinniped means "flipper feet."

Walruses have tusks.
The tusks are two long
teeth. They start growing
soon after the walrus
is born. Walruses use
their tusks to pull themselves
out of water and onto land.

The walrus has blubber
to keep it warm
in the cold water.
A baby walrus is small
and has just a thin layer
of blubber. It needs
its mother to keep warm.